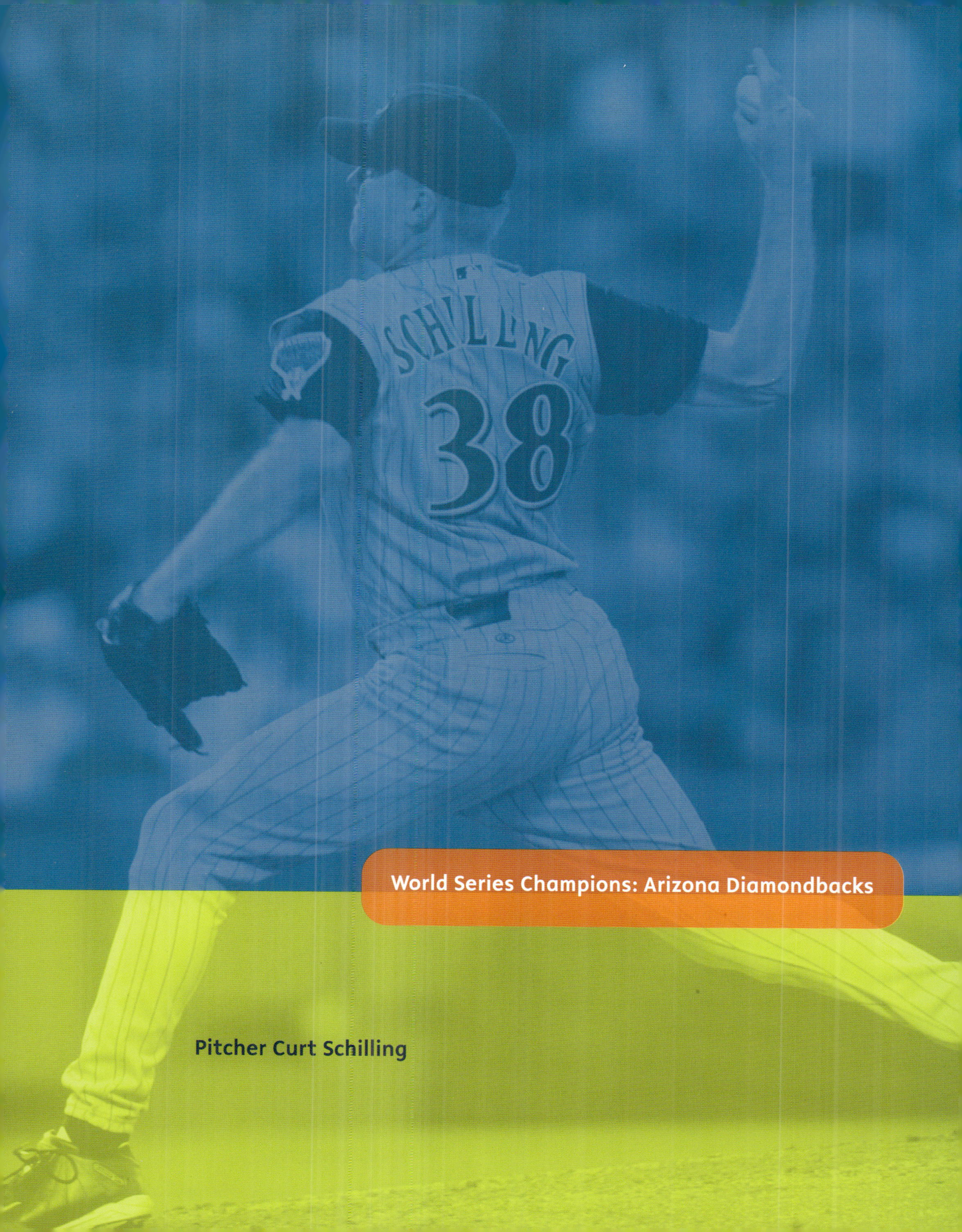

World Series Champions: Arizona Diamondbacks

Pitcher Curt Schilling

Outfielder David Peralta

WORLD SERIES CHAMPIONS

ARIZONA DIAMONDBACKS

MEGAN COOLEY PETERSON

CREATIVE SPORTS

CREATIVE EDUCATION / CREATIVE PAPERBACKS

Published by Creative Education and Creative Paperbacks
P.O. Box 227, Mankato, Minnesota 56002
Creative Education and Creative Paperbacks are imprints of
The Creative Company
www.thecreativecompany.us

Art Direction by Tom Morgan
Book production by Ciara Beitlich
Edited by Joe Tischler

Photographs by Alamy (Reuters), Associated Press (Margaret Bowles, David Zalubowski), Getty (Brian Bahr, Dustin Bradford, Stephen Dunn, Mike Fiala, Otto Gruele Jr., Norm Hall, Carmen Mandato, New York Daily News Archive, Denis Poroy, Matthew Stockman), Shutterstock (Sean Pavone)

Library of Congress Cataloging-in-Publication Data
Names: Peterson, Megan Cooley, author.
Title: Arizona Diamondbacks / Megan Cooley Peterson.
Description: Mankato, MN : Creative Education and Creative Paperbacks, 2024. | Series: Creative sports. World Series champions | Includes index. | Audience: Ages 7-10 | Audience: Grades 2-3 | Summary: "Elementary-level text and engaging sports photos highlight the Arizona Diamondbacks' MLB World Series win, plus sensational players associated with the professional baseball team such as Luis Gonzalez."-- Provided by publisher.
Identifiers: LCCN 2023008238 (print) | LCCN 2023008239 (ebook) | ISBN 9781640268142 (library binding) | ISBN 9781682773642 (paperback) | ISBN 9781640009844 (pdf)
Subjects: LCSH: Arizona Diamondbacks (Baseball team)--History--Juvenile literature. | World Series (Baseball)--History--Juvenile literature.
Classification: LCC GV875.A64 P47 2024 (print) | LCC GV875.A64 (ebook) | DDC 796.357/640979173--dc23/eng/20230330
LC record available at https://lccn.loc.gov/2023008238
LC ebook record available at https://lccn.loc.gov/2023008239

Printed in China

2001 World Series Champions

Pitcher Zac Gallen

CONTENTS

Home of the Diamondbacks

Arizona is a state in the western United States. It is home to the Grand Canyon and the Arizona Diamondbacks baseball team. The Diamondbacks swing their bats at a **stadium** called Chase Field in Phoenix. Fans call them the D-backs.

The Diamondbacks are a Major League Baseball (MLB) team. They are a member of the National League (NL) West **Division**. Their **rivals** are the Los Angeles Dodgers. All MLB teams try to win the World Series to become champions.

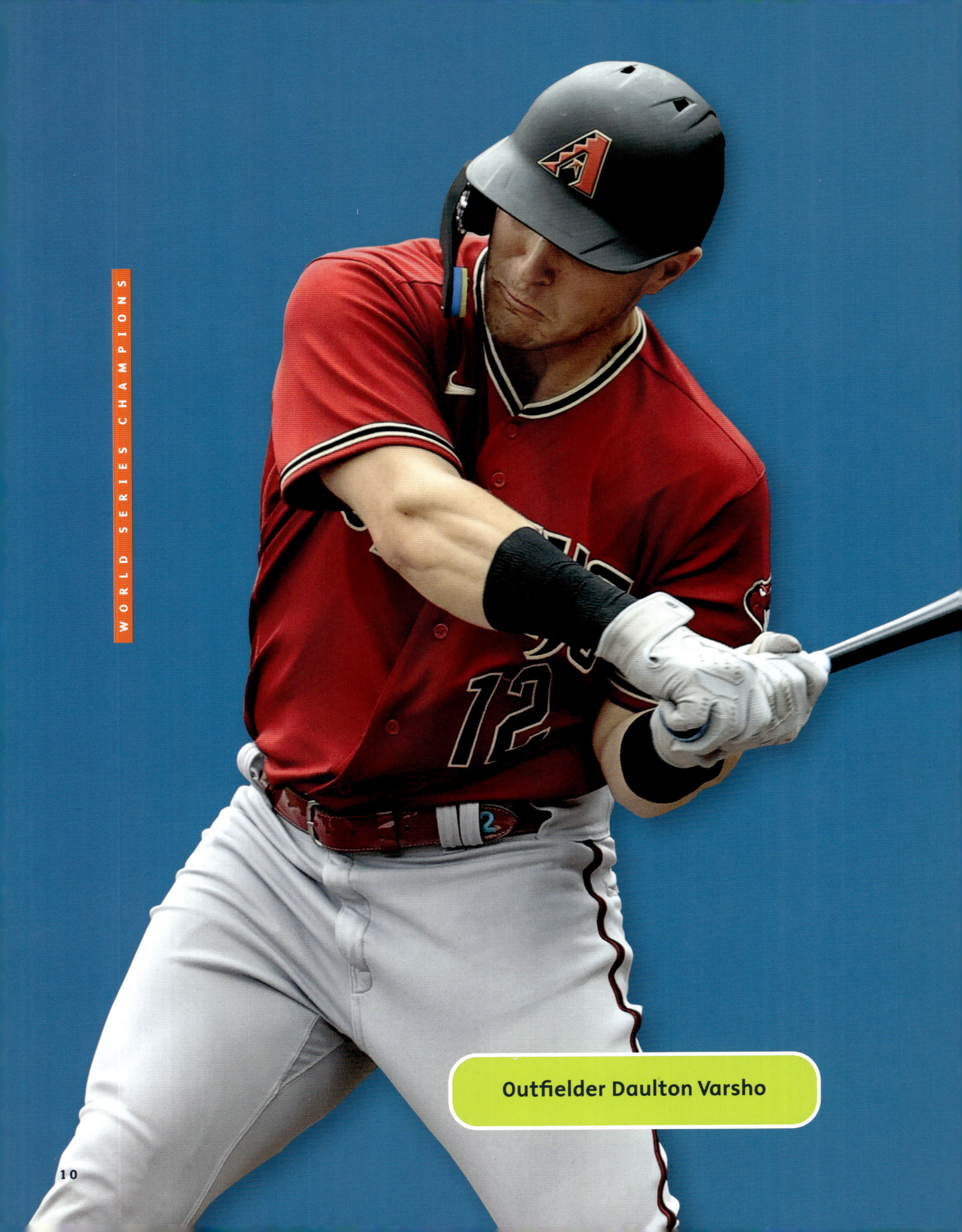

Outfielder Daulton Varsho

Naming the Diamondbacks

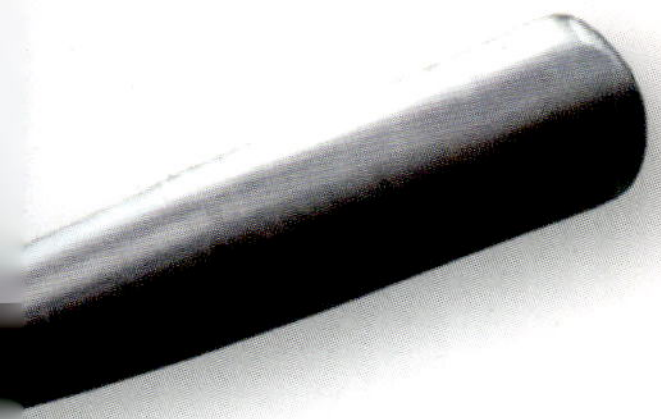

When they first formed, the team asked fans for help finding a name. Fans came up with the Rattlers, Scorpions, Phoenix, Coyotes, and Diamondbacks. Team leaders picked Diamondbacks. The diamondback is a rattlesnake found in Arizona. It has a diamond pattern on its body. The team plays on a baseball diamond. The D-backs wear red, black, and sand-colored uniforms.

Pitcher Andy Benes

Diamondbacks History

The Diamondbacks' first-ever game was in 1998. Travis Lee batted out hits. Right-hander Andy Benes struck out batters. More than 50,000 fans came out to watch the team run the bases.

The D-backs were winners right away. They won their division in just their second season. They have won five division titles so far.

Strong pitching shaped the Diamondbacks' early seasons. Randy Johnson won the Cy Young Award four times. This award is given to the season's best pitcher. Pitcher Curt Schilling went 4–0 in the **playoffs** in 2001.

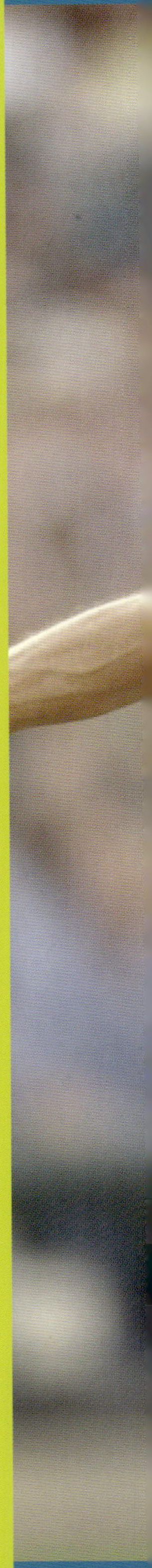

Pitcher Randy Johnson

Outfielder Luis Gonzalez

In 2001, the Diamondbacks faced the New York Yankees in the World Series. Star outfielder Luis Gonzalez had the game-winning hit in Game 7. The D-backs defeated the Yankees, 3–2. They were the world champions! Johnson and Schilling were named Most Valuable Players of the series. No other **expansion** team has won a World Series so quickly.

Other Diamondbacks Stars

The Diamondbacks found another great pitcher in Brandon Webb. He won the Cy Young Award in 2006. He also appeared in three straight All-Star Games.

Pitcher Brandon Webb

First baseman Paul Goldschmidt

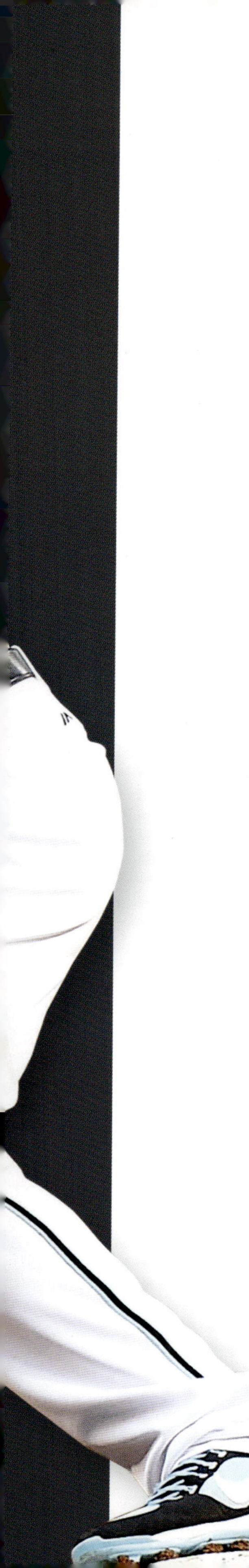

First baseman Paul Goldschmidt joined the team in 2011. He played in six straight All-Star Games. He won three Gold Gloves and four Silver Sluggers awards. The best fielders and hitters win them. He helped lead the D-backs to the playoffs in 2011 and 2017. Pitchers Zac Gallen and Joe Mantiply bring heat from the mound. Fans hope to see another championship in the Diamondbacks' future!

About the Diamondbacks

Started playing: 1998

League/division: National League, West Division

Team colors: red, black, and sand

Home stadium: Chase Field

WORLD SERIES CHAMPIONSHIPS:

2001, 4 games to 3 over New York Yankees

Arizona Diamondbacks website: www.mlb.com/dbacks

Glossary

division—a group of teams in a certain category for a competition

expansion—a new team in a sports league

playoffs—games that the best teams play after a regular season to see who the champion will be

rival—a team that plays extra hard against another team

stadium—a building with tiers of seats for spectators

Pitcher Joe Mantiply

Index